About the Author

Norma Fox Mazer is the author of SATURDAY, THE TWELFTH OF OCTOBER, a Lewis Carroll Shelf Award winner; A FIGURE OF SPEECH, a National Book Award finalist; DEAR BILL, REMEMBER ME? AND OTHER STORIES, an ALA Notable Children's Book; and THE SOLID GOLD KID, an ALA Best Book for Young Adults that was co-authored by her husband Harry Mazer. These books are available in Dell Laurel-Leaf editions. The Mazers live in Jamesville, New York.

Laurel-Leaf Books bring together under a single imprint outstanding works of fiction and non-fiction particularly suitable for young adult readers, both in and out of the classroom. Charles F. Reasoner, Professor of Elementary Education, New York University, is consultant to this series.

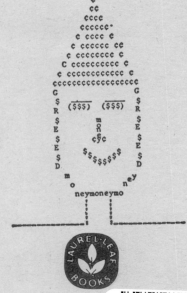

I, TRISSY

Norma Fox Mazer

*

Published by
Dell Publishing Co., Inc.
1 Dag Hammarskjold Plaza
New York, New York 10017

Laurel-Leaf Library ® TM 766734, Dell Publishing Co.,
Inc.

ISBN: 0-440-94142-3

RL: 5.2

Reprinted by arrangement with Delacorte Press

Printed in the United States of America

First Laurel-Leaf printing—May 1977
Second Laurel-Leaf printing—June 1978
Third Laurel-Leaf printing—June 1980

For my parents, Michael and Jean Fox

DECLARATION OF INDEPENDENCE

When in the curse of human events, it

becomes necess^rary for one people to

dissolve the plitical bandds which have

connected them with anothe%r, and to

assume among the powers of the eart.

...to assume among the powers of the

earth....

that's all I can remember power os

the earth duh duh dumb dumb

When in the course of human events, it

becomes necessary for one father to give

his daughtera typewriter...she knows

it's a bribe....

"Is this a bribe, Daddy?" I said.

"What do you mean by that, Trissy

Jane?" It's always Trissy Jane when he's

irritated, just Tris when he likes me.

"A bribe to keep my mouth shut," I
said.

"Your mouth shut? Why would I want
you to keep your mouth shut? Except for
the obvious reason that you do put your
foot in it an inordinate amount of the
time. But what is there to keep your
mouth shut about now?"

"You and Mom," I said. He just looked
at me. "Besides, you never brought us
presents before." When he was living
home with us, I meant. Just since he's
gone to live on his own, he brings
things all the time. This typewriter is
the biggest present I ever had. It
must have cost plenty! It's not a little

junky toy like I had last year.

The dumb thing is I loved this typewriter the minute I saw it. What Dad said when he gave it to me was, "Tris, now you can put down on paper all the things you're always making the mistake of saying out loud, and nobody has to know about them except you. It will probably make life pleasanter for everyone."

I wanted to kiss him and say thank you and all that, and instead I popped out with that about the bribe.

"Do you want me to return it?" Dad said.

"No."

"You sure?"

"Yes." I said it again, louder. "YES,
I'M SURE!" But I was still thinking it
was a bribe.

Hello, Bribe, ~~XXXXXXXXXXXXXXXXXXXXXX~~
                    my lfttle typewriter pet
hello, my little tyepwriter pet.
Don't get your feelings hurt. I do like
you. You're a sweet little black thing
with pretty silver keys, and it's not
your fault you're a bribe.

When Mother heard I'd said that about
a bribe (Blabbermouth Baby Boy Robert
told) she said that I oughtn't to look a
gift horse in the mouth. "Every little
extra helps now," she said. "Though he
might have been a lot more practical."
You can always count on Mother to say
something like that.

Also you can count on Mother to let
me know that BBB Robert "takes things"
better than I do, even if he is only six
plus eleven/twelfths, while I am
eleven plus six/twelfths.

She means about the separation. That's
what she said the day Daddy moved out.
I was over at Steffi's that afternoon,
and when I got home, Dad was gone, and
so was most of his stuff.

"We told you," Mother said. "We
prepared you. Now don't you start
getting sulky on me. You'll see your
father almost as much as you ever did,
I expect."

"Where is he? Why isn't he home?"

"Trissy! I'm going to scream if you

ask that once more. Your father and I

have explained this and explained this

to you and your brothers. You don't see

Mitch or Robert sulking, do you? Robert

is young, but he takes things one

hundred percent better than you do."

Mitch and Robert. Barf. Mitch takes

Mother's side on everything. And Robert

is so dumb he thinks it's FUN to see

Daddy just on Saturdays and go ~~places~~
every

places with him. Dad used to stick up

for me, but now he's gone. That's why

I got the typewriter, I guess.

                              I, Trissy

HELLO, TYPEWRITER

HOW YOU DOING?

HOW YOU KEEP YOUR LETTERS GROOVING?

I love to tip and type on my tapwriter
...I love the sound it makes click
click click clcik click click click
click click clock clickl clock clidk
click lick dlick click click click it
sounds so sleepy.....are you tired,
Typewriter?

WAKE UP, STUPID!

What should I write?

I want to write something, but I
don't have anything special to write.

Mrs. Gilfer in English class says
write anything that comes into your head
and pretty soon you will be writing

something that will surprise you. What

comes into my head? Nothing. I'm dumb.

I'm Steffi's best friend. I'm I'm I'm

Im Im.....bla blah blah....f is

my favorite letter...fffffffffffffffffff

cute little fff men all in a row...

also I like s, it's cozy and sleepy

sssssssssssss and snakey.....and o is

pretty cute itself oooooooooo all little

o faces, little o mouths, and little o

eyes so scared and small looking o, o,

o, oh, oh, oh! oh dear!

Oh dear, nighttime is near

Trissy my love you are so queer

My Gang!

I love me

And me loves me

And together the three of us

Play happily.

Trissy, Trissy, don't be late

Mom's in the kitchen till half past

eight

Little brother Robert licked your spoon

Big brother Mitch hit him with a broom

And poor Daddy won't be home tonight

Cause he can't stand the way we fight.

And now a station break, folks, with a

few words from our sponsor:

Are you hungry, thin, and

undernourished? Try NOURISHING

NUTRITIOUS TRISS GERM today. It's Chewy,

Crunchy, and Crispy. It's full of nuts.

Sprinkle some on your cream of wheat.

Mix it with your scrambled eggs. If you
have any left over, sprinkle it in your
bath water. Dissolves gritty grimy
greasy rings. Mothers love it!

(A Mother's voice:) "Sweetie, take
your Triss Germ, darling. It's going to
make you grow up to be strong and
healthy like Mommy, poopsie. Open your
mouth, Precious. Come on, Lover, take
your nice Triss Germ. Honey, you're
making Mommy just a teeny weeny bit mad,
Sweetums. Precious Lover, you're going
to make me scream. Darling....OPEN UP,
YOU ROTTEN LITTLE BEAST!"

> I TRISSY   I TRISSY
>
> I TRISSY   I TRISSY
>
> I TRISSY   I TRISSY

DINNER NEWS

We were at the table. Mother, Robert, Mitch, and me. Mitch sat down at Daddy's place. So I said, "Mitch, that's Daddy's place."

"Not any more," he said with a big Mouth Watering Grin.

"Move," I said.

Just gave me another MWG.

"MOVE!"

"Stop that, Trissy," Mother said. "Mitch can sit anywhere he wants."

"But he doesn't belong in that place." I was so mad I was practically jumping up and down.

"Don't raise your voice at me," Mother said. "You respect me. I'm your mother!"

"I'm your daughter! Why don't you respect me? Why don't you tell Mitch to get out of Daddy's seat? Why do you always get mad at me? Why is MITCH always right? Why am I always wrong? What's the answer?"

"You're rude, young lady! You leave the table and don't you come back till you are prepared to talk and act like a civilized person."

So I left. I pounded as I went up the stairs. I slammed the bathroom door as I passed. I slammed the door to my room so hard the mirror shook. Too bad it didn't fall and break into a thousand pieces.

Now my stomach is growling. SHE
wouldn't let me eat supper. SHE wouldn't
care if I died of starvation. Probably,
if SHE saw me crawling on the desert
with my bones sticking out of my
backside and my tongue hanging down to
my toes, SHE would only laugh.

Damn that Mitch.

Double damn him to hell and back.
Double damn them all, Mitch, Robert, and
HER. Double and triple and quadriple
DAMN them all. To Hell Hell Helly Hilly
Hollow Hellish Hell with them all!!!!!
!!
The I'll-be-glad-when-you're-dead,-
Mitch-Beers Smile:

```
          diediediediedie
          d ///////////// d
       i r            --  r i
      e  o   ha     ha   o  e
   d   p              p   d
    i   d              d   i
   e   a      &       a   e
       d    b   d        
       e     loo        e
       a              a
       deadeadeadeadead
          '        '
          '        '
         'r        '
```

```
        ha ha
           ha ha
              ha
              ha
              hahahahahahaha
```

I, Evil to the Heart, Trissy!!!!

TO WHOM IT MAY CONCERN

I, THE UNDERSIGNED, HENCEFORTH, WILL

SIT AT THE DINNER TABLE IN MY

DESIGNATED PLACE AND EAT MY DESIGNATED

FOOD WITH DESIGNATED SILVERWARE, AND

OTHERWISE CONDUCT MYSELF IN A POLITE,

PERFECT, AND IRREPROACHABLE MANNER.

EXCEPT THAT, I, THE UNDERSIGNED,

REFUSE NOW AND FOREVER, TO LOOK AT,

TALK TO, OR IN ANY WAY ACKNOWLEDGE THE

PRESENCE OR EXISTENCE OF ONE MITCH

BEERS, SO LONG AS HE, MITCH BEERS,

CONTINUES TO SIT IN THE PLACE OF MY

FATHER, MITCHELL POWELL BEERS.

I DO SO SOLEMNLY SWEAR.

I, TRISSY

QUESTIONS & ANSWERS

Mrs. Gilfer: Trissy, why do you sign all
your papers 'I, Trissy'?

Trissy: I like to.

Mrs. Gilfer: But why, Trissy? You
should sign your name
'Trissy Beers.'

Trissy: I like 'I Trissy' better.
Is it against the law or
something?

Mrs. Gilfer: Well, no, dear, and I do
like to allow for your
creative imagination to
take its own course, but it
is unusual. And then is it
grammatical? Well, I

believe it is, but it's a
redundancy, you know?

Trissy: I don't know what that is.

Mrs. Gilfer: It says the same thing
twice, Trissy. Ha ha, like
'Me, Jane.' That's a
redundancy, see?

Trissy: Oh! That's why you crossed
out 'huge, enormous
monster' on my tall tales
composition. But, anyway,
can I still sign my papers
the way I want to?

Mrs. Gilfer: Oh, dear. (She reached
inside her dress and
straightened her straps. Or
was it her false bosoms?

Everyone says she has them.) Yes, Trissy. You can still sign papers in my class 'I, Trissy,' but I don't know how your other teachers will take it. You see what I mean?

Trissy: Thank you, Mrs. Gilfer, I will meet that situation when it arises. (Which is what I heard Uncle Arthur say when he was visiting my mother.)

Mrs. Gilfer: My dear, that's very mature.

Question: Your name?

Answer: I, Trissy

*S*T*E*F*F*I*   *J*O*N*E*S*

HAS LO
    o
     o
      o
       o
        o
         o
          o
           o
            o
             o
              o
               o
                N G H
                   A
                    I
                     R
AND A teentiny NOSE

        AND A **************
               *   *
               * P*R*E*T*T*Y*   MOUTH
               *   *
               ****

STEFFI JONES THE TRULY BEAUTIFUL, AND

TRISSY BEERS THE TRULY BRILLIANT ARE

THE GREATEST FRIENDS IN THE WO WO WO

WORLD... IN THE SO SO SO SOLAR SYSTEM...

IN THE UNI UNI UNI UNIVERSE!!!!!!

he he he he he he hehehehehehehehehe

hehehehe LAURA STEGMEYER IS JEALOUS

ha ha ha ha ha ha hahahahahahahahahaha

hahahaha LAURA STEGMEYER KICKED TRISSY

BEERS IN THE LEG (didn't even hurt he

he) BECAUSE SHE IS SO GREEN EYED MONSTER

JEALOUS OF THE GREAT WONDERFUL TERRIFIC

FANTASTIC STAR SPANGLED

```
        *******************
        *                 *
        *F*R*E*N*D*S*H*I*P*
        *                 *
        *******************
```

OF STEFFI JONES AND TRISSY BEERS.

he ha he ha he ha hehahehahehahehaheha

ha ha TOO BAD FOR YOU, LAURA STEGMEYER.

THE ITMQ TEST

The ITMQ Test (The I, Trissy Mother's
Quotient Test, devised, designed, and
administered by TJB) may be filled out
by any certified child. Use a soft
pencil. Do not look at anyone else's
answers. Take 10 minutes. If you do not
understand a question, pass on to the
next one, and only return to the blanks
when you have completed all other
questions.

Answer yes or no to each of the
following questions, as it applies to
your mother. Does she:

XXXXXXXXXX	TRISSY	STEFFI
1- smoke?		
1- smoke?	yes	no
2- yell?	yes	no

	TRISSY	STEFFI
3- wear hair spray?	yes	no
4- wear heavy makeup?	yes	no
5- make packaged cakes?	yes	no
6- make unpleasant remarks to your father?	yes	no
7- favor one or more children above you?	yes	yes
8- fail to understand you?	yes	yes
9- get mad at you regularly?	yes	no
10- forget to rinse her mouth after she eats garlic pickles?	yes	no
11- wear her skirts too		

	TRISSY	STEFFI
short?	no	no

12- always flip off the
tv in the middle of
your favorite show,

| saying it is bedtime? | yes | no |

13- act helpless when
something goes wrong

| with the car? | yes | yes |

14- forget to come up lots
of nights to tell you

| goodnight? | yes | no |

15- tell you you're old
enough to know better
when you do something
wrong, but that you
are too young when you

want to do something

she doesn't want you

to do and doesn't

want to give the

reason for?   yes   yes

. . . .

Score 6 points for each NO answer. A

PERFECT ITMQ score is 90. This means you

are superior in your choise of mothers.

From 80-90: You are gifted in choice of

mother.

From 70-80: You are above average in

choice.

From 60-70: You fall in the average

range of mother-choosers.

From 50-60: Disappointing.

From 40-50: Clearly a failure in mother
            choice.

From 20-40: Cause for alarm!

From 10-20: The situation is grave!

From 0 -10: You poor kid! How did you
            do it?

MEMO TO MY MOTHER

(who recently got a score of 6 in the
ITMQ)

Below are a list of nine practical
suggestions to improve your ITMQ test
score and increase your chances of
persuading my father to come live with
us again. Please study each suggestion
carefully and ACT on it.

1 - Stop smoking like a chimney. Your
fingers and teeth are yellow, and that's
ugly. You are polluting your lungs, and
your children's air space, and that's
bad.

2 - Look interested when my father
tells stories. Don't get busy dusting or

yelling at us kids. You should have done that before. And don't walk out on him in the middle of a story. Practice in front of the mirror till you know how to look interested.

3 - Get sweeter. Practice by saying nice things to your daughter, such as: What a pretty smile!....Every day you grow more helpful!....I'm such a lucky mother to have a daughter like you!....

Instead of saying things like, I'm going to scream! Your hair looks like a rat's nest!....You could grow potatoes in those ears!....Your room isn't fit for a pig!

4 - Stop playing favorites with your children. Robert is NOT a baby anymore,

he's going to be seven, so stop calling him "the baby."

5 - Call up my father and tell him you're sorry. I don't know what for. Just tell him you're sorry for whatever it is you're sorry for. You must be sorry for something, otherwise he wouldn't have left us.

6 - Stop calling Mitch, "My big man." That's disgusting, since he's only 15 years old, and once I heard my father say you're going to get that boy all screwed up if you don't let him off your apron strings.

7 - Invite your husband to supper and make him a sensational meal. Not hamburgers slapped on the pan when he

walks in and frozen french fries in the oven, and you jumping around nervously saying, "Oh, I was so busy today, I didn't have time for anything."

8 - Bake a real cake. Not frozen strawberries glopped over store bought angel food cake that tastes like cotton. Make a real cake buried under tons of real whipped cream. Invite my father over to have coffee and cake. DON'T give Robert and Mitch bigger pieces than you give me.

9 - Last, but NOT least. Visit Steffi Jones' mother. Her mother is a real MOTHER. She is pretty, sweet, and loving. She bakes homemade cakes, smells good, and knows how to make EVERYBODY

feel good. When you visit Mrs. Jones,
watch EVERYTHING she does. Practice
acting like Mrs. Jones. Remember, MR.
Jones is living home with Mrs. Jones and
Steffi and her little sister Bea.

                    I, Trissy

AM I CREATIVE, OR FRIENDLY?

Mrs. Gilfer says, "Remember, ka-lass, kree-a-tive ex-presh-un in your compositions counts the most." She says the most kree-a-tive person in the ka-lass gets to be editor of our sixth grade yearbook.

That's sure to be Great Old Me, Beautiful Old Steffi, or (ugh) Laura Stegmeyer of the frizzy red hair.

On the playground, Ugh Stegmeyer told me I should let Beautiful Old Steffi win the contest Mrs. Gilfer opened today.

"You know how to use flashy words and will do something to draw attention to yourself," Ugh Stegmeyer said. "You say you're Steffi's best friend. Ha! You don't want her to be editor."

"It's up to Mrs. Gilfer, and depends on who's the most--"

"If _I_ was Steffi's best friend, I would GLADLY let her win. In fact, I'm not going to hand in my very best creative effort, so Steffi can have an extra good chance." She gave me her very best creative smile and walked away.

ugh ugh ugh ugh ugh ugh ugh ugh ugh!!!

NOTICE TO LAURA STEGMEYER

If you think you are going to get

between me and Steffi Jones by your

sneaky, insidious insinuations, you are

WRONG. If you think I am not going to

do my best CREATIVE effort in the

contest, you are WRONG AGAIN!!!!!!!!!!!!

I! Trissy!!!!!!!!

Mrs. Gilfer

English Class   I, Trissy

A ONCE UPON A TIME STORY

Once upon a time there lived a king and queen to whom a child was born. They named her Tolda. The king couldn't have been happier. The queen, however, couldn't be bothered, and gave the tiny princess entirely to the care of servants.

The queen was extremely high strung and screamed day and night at the king, her chief complaint being that he presented a shockingly poor image of a king. She criticized him for spending too little time sitting on the royal throne settling disputes and ordering people around. Furthermore, she accused him of being a cheapskate about keeping the royal wardrobe up to date. A real king, she scolded, didn't go around looking like a shabby last year's model.

The king, however, thought that the way he dressed was irrelevant as long as he was comfortable. And as far as the people were concerned, they didn't need to come running to him with every little problem. The king mimicked one of the supplicants.

"Oh, Dear King, Sir Lordship, Your Worship, Sir Kindness, Royal to the Highest, my father gave my brother two pairs of boots, and my brother won't share with me."

The king made a disgusted face. "Who wants to listen to a lot of boring boot licking speeches?" Besides, he said, his behind became quite numb sitting in one place for hours on _end_. "Get it!" the king chortled. "Hours on _end_!"

The queen sniffed. "You and your puns! You're a pitiful, pathetic example for the poor ignorant populace to look up to. Because of you they laugh at me!" By this time the queen had worked herself up into a fine frenzy. "Nobody respects me," she screamed. "I don't have enough money or jewels. My kingdom is filled with lazy slobs who throw stones at me when I go driving in the royal carriage."

"Now, my dear--"

"Don't you now-my-dear me, king! It's all your fault! You're not a proper king!"

"Now, Queen, don't get yourself all upset."

"'Now, Queen! Now, Queen!' Ooooh, you miserable king, you make me so angry!"

Bang! Slam! Smash! The queen didn't care who heard her kicking the royal footstools, slamming doors, and stamping her royal feet in a rage.

Nothing satisfied her. She sat on her royal throne and tapped her foot irritably. She sent the servants scurrying from one end of the palace to the other on silly errands. She was

displeased with everything and everyone.
When her daughter Tolda appeared,
running to kiss her mother, the queen
gnashed her teeth and said, "You're too
old for that sentimental kissing stuff!"
The only person who pleased her was Sir
Arthur Suckapipe, the queen's minister,
who stood behind her throne, whispering
in her ear.

It was Sir Arthur Suckapipe who gave
the queen the idea that nothing ought to
satisfy her till the king won back from
the people the respect, admiration, and
fear the throne deserved.

A war, said the queen, (with Sir
Arthur Suckapipe nodding behind her) was
the thing to unite the kingdom and

restore respect for the king and queen.
There was nothing like killing the
enemy to make the throne popular and the
people happy.

The king was thoroughly disgusted with
this idea. He didn't want his name
connected with killing and bloodshed.
There had been too much of that gory
stuff, he said, committed in the name
of kings, kingdoms, and royal causes.

"In that case," the queen said, "you
have to set out on a long treacherous
mission to find something."

"Find what, my dear?"

"How should I know?" she screamed.
"That's your business. Surely there
must be something you can go out and
seek!"

The king poo-pooed the idea that there was anything beyond the kingdom that he or any of his people needed or wanted. "We have everything close at hand to be happy," he said.

The queen stamped her foot. "You silly man!"

Day after day she nagged him mercilessly. "You lazy, stay-at-home, ambitionless, big bottomed, spineless king without a backbone! You don't deserve the name of king!"

Finally the king became so disgusted he packed up and left. When people asked where he had gone, the queen put on her most mouth watering grin and said he had set out on a holy journey to unknown lands to win new riches and glory for their kingdoms. "Oh! Ah! How wonderful!" everyone said.

Poor Tolda. Now that her father was gone, her life became poor indeed. The queen now forced her to do palacework, spending long hours on her hands and knees mopping the mile long white marble corridors. Meanwhile the queen and Sir Arthur smiled and whispered together.

So it went for many months. Tolda grew thin and weak, her knees were red and knobby, but still she slaved. Every night she prayed for her father's safe return. Often she cried herself to sleep.

Then a strange sickness swept over the kingdom. Many people died. People whispered it was a punishment because the king was gone. They stood outside the palace, calling for the return of the king. The queen appeared in the royal robes, her crown tipsy because she had put it on in such a hurry. But the people were angry. They threw mud, stones, and slop at her. They wanted the king.

The queen was afraid. The sickness had swept to the gates of the royal household. She locked the palace doors, dismissed the gatekeeper and most of the servants. Tolda was ill and so was Sir

Arthur Suckapipe. Alone and afraid, the
queen shivered.

First Sir Arthur Suckapipe died. Then
Tolda was taken. The queen was beside
herself with remorse and grief. Now that
it was too late, the queen tore her hair
because she had been so wickedly unkind
to her own dearest daughter.

But Tolda wasn't dead. Weak, her
breath almost gone, she had been carried
away by the faithful gatekeeper to a hut
at the edge of a meadow where his old
mother treated her with herbs and
brought her back to life.

The queen, meanwhile, grew more and
more fearful and suspicious. The people
were whispering about her. There were

rumors of a plot afoot to oust her from
the throne and lock her in the Purple
Tower. She was sorry now she'd driven
the king away. She had new locks put on
every royal door, and she allowed no one
but herself to hold the keys. She rarely
went out, but crept about the palace
muttering to herself and peering through
the cracked windows at the people
outside.

One day a ragged, bearded beggar
appeared at the palace gates. The doors
were locked and padlocked. There was no
gatekeeper to let him in. And when he
turned to the people and said he was
their king, they laughed. Everyone knew
the king was dead, and only a mad queen
dwelt within the palace.

The queen, hearing the beggar

hammering on the ~~xxx~~ royal gates,
her
dragged heavy wooden tables and chairs

to pile against the doors, sure the

revolt had begun. Thinking of her own

precious head chopped off, she shivered

in fear.

The king circled the palace walls.

There was no response from the palace.

In despair, he turned away. It was then

the faithful gatekeeper found him and

brought him to Tolda. There was a

tearful reunion. The king showed Tolda

the treasures he'd brought back, sewn in

the lining of his coat. He showered

diamonds, gold bracelets and silver

necklaces on her.

Together, wearing their new treasure, they returned to the palace, raised up on the shoulders of the happy people. The queen heard the turmoil at the gates, and peering through the crack in the great door all she saw was a huge mass of shrieking, clamorous people. With a last scream, she dropped dead.

After that, the king ruled his kingdom wisely and well with Tolda at his side.

The end

I, Trissy

MY MOTHER, THE SPY

She met me at the door when I got
home. "I found this paper on your desk."

"What paper? Oh. That paper."

She said, "Nine practical suggestions
to improve yourself!" She was furious.
She shook the paper at me. "'Your
fingers are yellow.' Thanks, so much, my
darling daughter! 'Get sweeter.' How
good of you to give me suggestions for
self improvement. I'll be ever lastingly
GRATEFUL! Now what do you have to SAY
for yourself?"

"You weren't supposed to read it."

"Oh, no! I thought it was written for
my <u>benefit</u>. And you thoughtfully left it

right smack on your desk so I could find
it EASILY!"

"My desk is private. You had no
business snooping--"

WHAM! She caught me across the face.
"Don't you call me a snoop besides
everything else, Trissy Beers." Her
voice was high and shaking. My cheek
stung, and I wanted to cry, but I hated
her so much I grinned instead. I grinned
so hard my jaw ached. She had no right
snooping. It was just something to write
on my typewriter. It was my personal
business.

From now on I NEVER leave anything on
my desk, EVER AGAIN.

                              I, TRISSY

RASPUTIN, I LOVE YOU

I wore my red cape to school today.

Mr. Montgomery asked me if I was
practicing to be Superwoman. "No.
Superman," I said.

Everybody laughed. Mr. Montgomery
didn't like that. He likes to make the
jokes. He will get back at me for having
made everybody laugh, I know that. He's
got mean eyes, but I like his class
anyway. He's always telling us bloody
stories about history. He says all of
history is written in a river of blood.

"Picture the crucified men lining the
road to Rome," he says, walking up and
down in front of the class. "Do you
think Jesus was the first or only man

crucified? Fat chance. In those days they really knew how to punish. They'd been practicing for thousands of years, beating, maiming, enslaving other people."

He says people used to have their hands chopped off for stealing, their ears slashed away, their noses clipped, and their eyes gouged out. He points his finger. His mean little eyes sparkle. He wakes everybody up. Nobody sleeps in Mr. Montgomery's class.

My favorite story is one he told about Rasputin, the mad monk of Imperial Russia. His enemies wanted to kill him. They got together and poisoned his food. They were there as he ate the poisoned food. They must have been rubbing their hands together. But old Rasputin went on eating and talking. They got so mad they shot him, but he still went on living, staggering around and frightening them. Then they strangled him. He was covered with blood and gore, but still alive, gasping for breath, his huge hypnotic eyes fixed accusingly on his assassins. They were terrified. He was supposed to have supernatural powers. They began to think he would never die. Finally they threw him into the river with weights tied to his body, and even then he sank so slowly they thought any moment he would come bobbing to the surface to accuse them.

Wow.

TYPING PRACTICE

I will now type all the words I can
type using just my left hand...on my
mark...get set...go!

eat ate cat rat sat sex car care west
waste wad wax ax fact ass fate feet fat
fast reed deed seed fart

Okay, right hand--go!

up pop pip pom pony poppy poop loop
lip jim mop mom join john mill milk

Robert is pounding on the wall. That
means my typewriter is bothering him.
Well, too bad for little BBB Robert, my
typewriter is mine own and it was given
me by mine own Dad, and I can type on it
all night if I wish, and you, old

Robert boy, can just take your little
bawling blabby baby self and bawl and
blab to Mom and see where that will get
you.

Here she comes now.

Well, I will just pretend I don't
hear or notice anything, and just go on
typing my fastest, with my best, most
concentrated, serious working
expression, and let her stand in the
doorway and be mad. Sputter ~~Suppter~~
Suppter
sputter. What does it matter to me? Ha
ha the Mad Typist of Free America can
not be stopped. I can type all day
and type all night. I can type till my
fingers fall off, and then for spite
I'll still type on with my bloody

stumps. Ha ha the Mad Typist strikes

again. drip

dr
$_i$
p dr
$_i$
p (blood)

SOME BOYS ARE IDIOTS AND I HAVE THE PROOF

John Rickover came up to me on the playground today and said, "Is your name Beers?" He was finishing an ice cream pop.

"Yes, it is. Is your name Rickover?"

"You mean like Budweiser Beer?"

"No. Beers. B-e-e-r-s."

"Oh, bears," he said, making paws and growling at me.

"No, BEERS."

"You mean bare. BARE," he shouted. "B-A-R-E." He began dancing around me like an idiot, shouting, "Trissy Bare. Bare Trissy, Trissybare Trissybare.

B! A! R! E! Bare BARE! BARE! BARE
NAKED!"

I snatched the ice cream pop from his
hand and jammed it into his mouth so
hard I thought his eyes would pop out of
his head. He spit it out and socked me
in the shoulder. I charged him and
butted him in the belly. The next
minute, Mr. Patterson, the playground
director, came flying over, his long
legs churning and pulled the two of us
apart. Then he gave ME a lecture.
"You're a girl. Girls aren't supposed
to fight with boys--"

"Tell HIM that!" I felt like kicking
Mr. Patterson in the leg. Maybe he read
my mind. The next thing I knew I was in

the principal's office, and the

secretary was sighing, "What is it this

time, Miss Trissy Trouble?"

DEAR BLABBY,

I am always getting into trouble and
lately it's worse than ever. Can you
help me improve myself? My mother says I
absolutely must learn to control my
worst impulses. My father says I need
to think twice before I speak once. And
my brother Mitch says I ought to nail
my feet to the floor and my mouth shut.

Right now it is Saturday. It's the day
I'm supposed to spend with my father,
but I am a prisoner in my room while my
goody goody brothers are out with Daddy.
This is my punishment for what I did
yesterday on my brother Robert's
birthday.

It started out to be a good day. After

school Mom baked a cake for Robert instead of buying it at the Buttercup Bakery like she usually does. It was a chocolate cake (my favorite) and it looked great in the oven. After she took it out, though, the center caved in. My brother Mitch said that crater or not, it was still better than any cake she could have bought.

"Do you really mean that, Mitch?" my mother said. "Just say the word--I'm ready to throw it away. I honestly am."

"Oh, no, it's great. It tastes great. Go ahead and frost it," Mitch said.

You notice she didn't ask my opinion, which I would have been happy to give. But for once Mitch was right and not

just apple polishing like crazy. And
anyway, she let me make the frosting and
even when it came out kind of thin and
sticky, she said it was great. I mean,
it was really getting to be a good day,
even if Robert did keep pestering
everybody, "What'd you get me? Something
that cost a lot of money, I hope?"

Mom stuck seven candles in the cake,
took a roast beef out of the oven, and
we all sat down to eat. By all, I mean
my mother, my brothers, me, and Uncle
Arthur. He's not our real uncle, but Mom
says calling him just plain Arthur is
disrespectful, and Mr. Jobaggy is too
formal. It's a good thing we don't have
to call him Mr. JOBAGGY, because

everytime I say Mr. JOBAGGY, I want to
laugh.

Mr. JOBAGGY used to visit us sometimes
before my father left. Once I heard
Daddy call him every woman's handy
neighborhood bachelor. My father thought
that was very funny, but my mother said
it was in poor taste. Anyway, now he's
at our house almost every week, and
we're supposed to be very polite to him
at all times.

I don't mind being polite (when I can
remember) but when Mom put Uncle Arthur
in my father's place at the table, it
got me even madder than when my brother
Mitch sat there. She didn't have to be
that polite and friendly.

My mother has been pretty mad at me
for quite a long time, and I didn't want
to make her mad again, so I kept my lips
sealed. I thought of all the tortures in
the world that would happen to me if I
said anything about MR. JOBAGGY sitting
in my father's place. I thought of
Chinese water torture, hanging by my
thumbs, being pulled apart limb from
limb on a medieval rack, and being
pierced by steel spikes inside the iron
lady.

"What's wrong with you, Trissy?" my
mother said. "You're just picking at the
food. Don't you like the meat? I thought
rare red roast beef was your favorite."

"It's delicious," Uncle Arthur said.

"I'll take another thick, bloody piece, Edith."

"Pass Uncle Arthur the meat, Mitch," Mom said. Mitch sneered as he passed the meat. About the only thing Mitch and I agree on is Uncle Arthur. We don't like him. He drawls out his words, and takes forever to say anything. "That's an in-ter-est-ing prob-lem," he says. And he acts so wise and judicious. "Let's look at the other side of the question," he says. Which is supposed to be some kind of wonderful, fantastic FAIR attitude to have. Personally, I like people to have opinions.

And my opinion was that it was WRONG for Uncle Arthur to be sitting in my

father's place, and WRONG for my father
to be absent on Robert's birthday. I
was getting madder and madder at
everyone, even Robert for being so
greedy and dumb that he didn't even know
it was wrong to have his birthday
without our father.

"You're still not eating, Trissy,"
Mom said. She got her suspicious look,
which is a sort of pinching around her
nose. "Did you eat a lot of sweets and
junk at school today?"

All of a sudden I made up my mind to
call my father. I pushed away my plate
and got a sick look on my face. That
wasn't too hard. I just stared at that
oozing roast beef and thought about

having my eyes pulled dripping and
bloody from their sockets.

"I have to go to the bathroom," I
said. I was gagging. "In a rush!"

I went into the bathroom, spit into
the sink, and then sort of quietly went
into my mother's room. I sat on the edge
of her bed, put the phone on my lap, and
dialed my father's new number. A girl
answered.

"Who are you?" I said.

"Excuse me?"

"Is this Professor Beers' residence?"

"Yes, it is," she said.

"I want to talk to him, please." I
decided she was probably one of my
father's students. My father is a

physicist at the University, and besides
teaching, he does research, and when he
was living home his students used to
visit him a lot.

"Hello, Tris!" he said. Just hearing
his voice gave me happy shivers.

"Hello, Daddy. Can you come over to
the house now? Please. Mother wants you
to." I had all my fingers and both legs
crossed.

"What for, Tris? I'm sort of busy. I
have company--"

"Well, there's something going on, and
she wants you here, because it's this
family thing--"

"You mean Robert's birthday?"

"Yes, that's right. Robert's birthday.

Mom baked a cake and we're all eating
now. You've got time to get here before
Robert cuts the cake and opens his
presents--"

"Well, Tris, the thing is--why? We're
going to celebrate Robert's birthday
again, when I see you kids tomorrow. I
have a pretty nice special treat planned
for you and your brothers. Your mother
and I agreed--"

"Robert wants you," I said. "He wants
you so bad, he's crying. He's really
crying hard."

"You mean Robert is _crying_?" Dad said.

"Yes. He's crying BUCKETS! I feel so
sorry for him." I got tears in my eyes.
I get that way when I tell a story. It

seems so real to me, I forget I'm making it all up. "The worst thing is, Mom is getting mad at him for ruining his birthday celebration. She spent a lot of time baking a real cake, and now he's acting so sad and babyish because you're not here."

Dad must have put his hand over the phone because I didn't hear him breathing or anything for a minute. Then he came back again and said, "Okay, I'll be right over, Tris. You tell Robert I'll be right over and to stop crying. In about ten, fifteen minutes, okay?"

I went back to the table. I felt sort of tense at what I'd done. Mom frowned. "Where were you so long, Trissy?"

Because of Uncle Arthur, she kept her voice sweet. "Were you in the bathroom all this time?"

"I thought you fell in," Mitch said.

"And got flushed away," Robert yelled.

"Oh, boy, funn-y," I said.

I was getting to feel more and more peculiar thinking about what I'd done, about Dad's coming over, and how surprised everyone was going to be, especially Mom. She kept giving me these penetrating looks, which meant she was wondering if my stomach was still upset. Usually when I stay in the bathroom too long, she wants to know if I am all right, or if I have cramps, and did I have a normal movement.

And if I didn't, then out comes the stuff which gets you tightened right up. I hate it. It tastes like chalk, but Mom always makes me take four huge tablespoonsful which make me feel sicker than any cramps. Anyway, I think it is disgusting that a person my age still has to answer humiliating personal questions.

My stomach had been growling and working ever since I made the phone call. Suddenly I burped. It was very loud, like this UUURRRP and came so fast I didn't have time to cover my mouth.

Mom gave me a freezing what-horrible-manners look. Mitch snickered in a superior way even though he burps all

the time himself, and MUCH louder and
more vulgar than I could hope to be.
(He wins every burping contest hands
down.)

About then, Dad walked in. "Why,
Mitchell," my mother said. "What are you
doing here? I thought we agreed you'd
call before you came over--"

When my father and Uncle Arthur saw
each other, both their faces got red and
stiff. "What do you mean?" my father
said. "Trissy called me and said you
wanted--" He looked at Robert. "She
said the boy was crying for me."

Everyone looked at me.

"I think I'll go to the bathroom," I
said.

"Sit down!" my mother ordered.

"I wasn't crying," Robert said. "Why would I cry? It's my birthday, and I'm happy because I'm getting a big bunch of presents that cost a lot of money."

"Just exactly what did you have in mind, Trissy?" my mother said.

"You lied to me," Daddy said. "Robert wasn't crying."

"Me cry? I never cry," Robert said cheerfully.

"Don't you think 'lie' is a little strong, Mitchell?" Uncle Arthur said. "She's only a child. Her motives, I'm sure, were well intended--"

"Keep out of this," my father said. "What are you doing here anyway?" Uncle

Arthur stood up. Then my father said,

"Oh, forget it, will you, Art?"

"Honestly!" my mother said.

"Honestly!" I couldn't tell if she was

madder at me or at my father.

"Well, Dad," Mitch said, "why don't

you sit down, now that you're here, and

have cake with us, anyway?" I almost

fell off my chair. For once in my life I

could have kissed old Mitch, even if he

is 15, and you know that is a smelly age

for boys. I mean, their underarm

perspiration odor is enough to knock

you dead at 20 paces.

Dad sat down. Robert made his greedy,

dollar sign face and asked if Dad had

brought his birthday present. Mom

ordered me to clear the plates and wipe
the table. She brought in the cake.
Uncle Arthur clapped. No one else did.

Robert couldn't blow out the candles
alone, and Mitch and Dad and Uncle
Arthur all had to help him. "All
together now," Uncle Arthur said. "One
big blow!" Out went the candles and
everyone started talking, while Robert
ripped open his presents.

"Happy Birthday, Robert," I a yelled,
thinking that people weren't ad mad at
me anymore.

But parents never forget. My
punishment for lying to Dad, deceiving
Mom, and generally being disruptive is
not being allowed to go out with my

father today and being confined to my room all day. My parents agreed on this punishment. I think it's fantastically dumb that the ONLY thing they have actually agreed on in months is how terrible I am, and what my punishments should be. But when I tried to say so, Mom told me I'd said enough and more than enough.

I have tired out my fingers, but made two hours pass writing all this to you, Dear Gabby, and now my fingers are just going by themselves, and they are almos nummmm now and i am tootired to use capitolletters anymore and i gess i will strt shrt handng all mi splng becuz it

is 2 much trbl 2 kp rting evree thng
out

i evn hav 2 lok back 2 rembr wat my
kweshtun wuz. sumthng abot beng a betr
persn. do u thnk u can anser that nd
also giv me sum pontrs on kping out of
trbl?

sinfly yrs

don in the moth

i trissy

MY BROTHER ROBERT'S GREEDY BIRTHDAY FACE

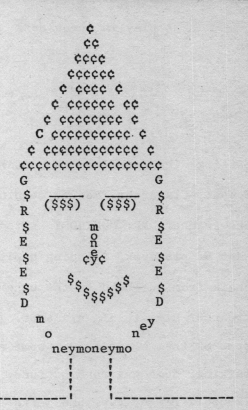

RED, WHITE, & BLUE

A play in three acts

by

T. J. Beers

ACT I

Setting: The Jefferson Elementary School

Scene: Classroom, Monday morning.

The teacher, MR. MONTGORY, sits on the edge of his desk, flipping a piece of chalk from one hand to the other. In front of him sit his students. That is, some of them are sitting, some are talking, some are reading funny books. The bell rings. Everyone jerks to attention. In the front row sits MELISSA SNEERS. Next to her, her best friend, STEFFI PRETTY. Directly behind Steffi

Pretty sits Melissa Sneers worst, most hated enemy, LIAR STEWMIAR.

Melissa Sneers is wearing a navy blue skirt, white blouse, red cape, and one red sock, one white sock. Melissa Sneers has a reason for dressing this way. Over the weekend, Melissa was severely and unjustly punished by her cruel guardians. Now she is protesting. Red stands for anger. White for innocence, and blue for unjust punishment.

Melissa sits with the cape wrapped around herself. She is behaving perfectly, bothering no one with her silent red, white, and blue protest.

MR. MONTGORY: Melissa Sneers, remove your cape.

MELISSA: (standing) I don't wish to

                 remove my cape, Mr.

                 Montgory.

(Melissa is utterly polite. Everyone in

the class sits up and watches. They

now expect some fun from Mr. Montgory,

who is renowned for his sarcastic

manner.)

MR. MONTGORY: Miss Sneers, if it is not

                 too much trouble, I expect

                 you to comply with my

                 orders in this classroom.

                 Now, if Miss Sneers does

                 not mind walking back to

                 the cloak room, I and all

                 the others in this class

                 would be most appreciative

> if Miss Sneers removed her
> cape and hung it with
> other garments designed
> for wear OUTSIDE the
> classroom.

(Appreciative snickers from the
students. Melissa bravely holds her
ground and her cape.)

MR. MONTGORY: Melissa Sneers, you are
being DISRUPTIVE!

MELISSA: (aghast at such
unfairness) Mr. Montgory,
would you say I was being
disruptive if I had a
flag?

MR. MONTGORY: I don't see what that has
got to do with anything,
Miss Sneers!

MELISSA: If I had a flag, it would
be the same colors as the
colors I am wearing, and
everybody would stand
and salute.

(At this, John Lickover stands and
salutes Melissa Sneers. All students
scream with laughter, except Steffi
Pretty, who looks very pale, ladylike,
and angry with her best friend, Melissa
Sneers, for causing such a commotion.)

MR. MONTGORY: Melissa Sneers, do you
refuse to take off your
cape?

MELISSA: (bravely) Yes, Mr.
Montgory, I refuse.

MR. MONTGORY: Miss Sneers, I will give

you one more chance! Take
off your cape!

MELISSA: Mr. Montgory, if I take

off my cape, I will take

off my skirt and blouse

also, because they are an

outfit and all three go

together.

(At this, boys stamp their feet and
laugh, girls giggle, and Steffi Pretty
looks even paler and angrier.)

MR. MONTGORY: Melissa Sneers, go to the

office IMMEDIATELY!

(Melissa Sneers exits, proudly holding
the red cape around herself. Students
look after her, buzzing. Mr. Montgory
raps on desk for order.)

Curtain falls.

ACT II

Setting: Office of the Principal of
Jefferson Elementary school. There is a
barred window over the reception desk.
Several student prisoners sit on a bench
waiting for their cases to be called.
They are a tough looking bunch. Into
their midst comes Melissa Sneers with
her red cape sailing behind her.
Everyone gasps at the bold, striking
picture she makes as she sits down.
Much whispering behind hands. They are
pointing her out as the girl who defied
Mr. Montgory and threatened to take off
her blouse and skirt in his class.

SECRETARY: (looking disapprovingly

                  through the barred

window) You may go in

now, Melissa Sneers.

(Melissa rises and sweeps her cape about

her. The door to the Principals's Office

swings silently open. Melissa enters.)

Curtain falls.

ACT III, Scene I

Setting: (That same afternoon.) Girls

Locker Room. Melissa Sneers, Steffi

Pretty, Liar Stewmiar in blue gym suits,

ready to enter gym.

LIAR STEWMIAR: Well, Melissa? What

happened? What did Mr.

Anderwert say? What's he

going to do to you?

MELISSA: Do? We talked for a

while. I explained the

situation, and he agreed
it's my right to dress
the way I want to. He
gave me permission to
wear my cape in school.

(Liar and Steffi gasp.)

LIAR STEWMIAR: You must be lying!

MELISSA: (coldly) I never lie. I
always tell the utter
truth!

STEFFI PRETTY: Well, I think you made a
fool of yourself in class
today! Come on, Liar.

(She and Liar link arms and leave for
gym, leaving Melissa behind.)

Curtain falls.

ACT III, Scene 2

Setting: The gymnasium. Parallel bars.

A rope hanging from the ceiling. It is

Melissa Sneers' turn to climb the rope.

MR. MUSCLES, the gym teacher, blows his

whistle.

MR. MUSCLES: Halfway up the rope,

girls!

(Steffi Pretty and Liar Stewmiar have

just come down and are standing

together, rubbing their sore hands and

arms. Melissa Sneers starts up the

ropes. She gets to the halfway mark.)

MR. MUSCLES: That's just fine,

Melissa. You can come

down now.

(Melissa keeps going, hand over hand,

feet clutching the rope. Up, up, and up
to the very top, where she dangles with
one hand as the entire girls' sixth
grade class gasps in disbelief.)

MR. MUSCLES: Terrific, Melissa! Girls,
                all you girls, look at
                Melissa. Look at what any
                of you girls could do if
                you tried harder. Great,
                Melissa! Okay, come on
                down now.

(Melissa slides down the ropes. Steffi
Pretty comes up to her as they are
lining up for the next exercises.)

STEFFI PRETTY: What's the matter with
                you, Melissa Sneers?
                You are getting

unbelievable, lately.

You are such a showoff,

I can't stand it. Do you

have to show off for

EVERY man teacher in the

WHOLE school?

LIAR STEWMIAR: (who has listened to

everything) She can't

help it. She's crazy. I

mean, MAN crazy.

(Liar Stewmiar and Steffi Pretty giggle.
Melissa pretends she doesn't care. She
smiles hard at Steffi Pretty. Melissa's
stomach grumbles and growls. Suddenly a
burp comes into Melissa's throat. She
tries to hold it back. She can't. She
burps loudly.)

STEFFI PRETTY: You're disgusting!

(Steffi Pretty and Liar Stewmiar put their arms around each other. Melissa Sneers, standing alone, looks sadly after them.)

Curtain falls.

The end.

HOW TO GET LOST, FIND A NEW FRIEND,

AND MAKE YOUR ENTIRE FAMILY FURIOUS

Saturday, when Daddy picked us up, he
hugged me, so I knew he wasn't mad about
Robert's birthday anymore. And he had me
sit in front next to him, with Mitch and
Robert in back. Robert was jumping
around and talking, but Mitch was
sitting in the corner, looking out the
window with his chin in his hands,
looking gloomy and stiff like he hated
being in the car with Dad. And when Dad
talked to him, Mitch kept answering
everything with one word.

"Well, Mitch, how was school this
week?"

"Okay."

"Okay. What do you mean by that? Did you keep up with all your classes this week?"

"Sorta."

"Well, how about math? You're taking eleventh grade math this year, right?"

"Yeah."

"Well, how's that going?"

"Okay."

"That's trig, isn't it?"

"Yeah."

"Trig's not easy."

"Yeah."

"You've got to keep up with the work, not fall behind."

"Uh-huh."

"Are you having any trouble with this, Mitch?"

"Nuh."

And so on like that, with Mitch just grunting out one word answers. Mean, just plain mean. When Daddy asked me about school, I told him everything I could think of, even about Mrs. Gilfer and her false bosoms. Dad laughed and glanced back at Mitch. Old Happy Face didn't even crack a smile. I was really mad at him. We only see our father once a week, so it's just mean of Mitch to act like a grim old grouch head.

At the museum, where Daddy took us, Mitch didn't act any nicer. He leaned against the wall and yawned and yawned. Robert ran up and down the spiral ramp, and Dad and I looked at the pictures.

Almost every weekend Dad brings us to the museum. It's getting kind of boring, but I wouldn't hurt his feelings by saying so. Some of the pictures are really weird. There's one that's purple and green and goes in and out as you watch it. It's the design that gives you that feeling, Dad said. When you turn away, you've got purple and green spots in front of your eyes, and everything's going in and out, in and out, like a swinging door. It's one of my favorite pictures.

"I guess Mitch is bored," Dad said as we went on to another picture.

"This is _fun_," I said. Dad put his arm around my shoulder. "I _love_ the museum,"

I said. "Let's not miss a single
Saturday!"

"Well, sure, if that's the way you
feel, Tris. But right now, I think we
better find something to do that Mitch
likes, also."

Dad motioned to the door, and Mitch
sort of slouched out after us. "What
now?" he said, sounding like he was
ready to pass out from boredom.

"I was thinking--maybe the boat show
at the War Memorial?" Dad said.

"Yeah. Three cheers for the boat
show," Robert yelled.

"I don't like boat shows," I said.
Dad wasn't listening. He was watching
Mitch.

"That's a pretty good idea," Mitch said, like he was a prince, handing out a favor to a mere subject.

"I thought you'd go for the boat show," Dad said with a happy look on his face. Mitch had wanted a sailboat for years. Before he left us, Dad said he might get our family a sailboat this summer.

"I don't like boat shows," I said again. But Mitch and Dad were already leading the way to the War Memorial. Robert was running around them, shooting his finger at the pigeons bobbing around on the sidewalk. Robert thinks it's funny to scare them up into the air. I told him pigeons have feelings, too, and maybe even have nervous

breakdowns from being scared by dumb

kids who yell at them and scatter them.

"Huh, Smarty," he said, "what about

cars? They make a trillion times more

noise than I do."

I walked behind him. The sun was hot.

The sidewalk was gritty and cruddy. I

had this peculiar itching feeling all

over. Dad and Mitch turned the corner.

Robert followed them. Dad had his arm

around Mitch's shoulder, and they were

walking in step. I kept walking along,

looking down at the sidewalk. If you

look carefully, you can see lines and

tracks all over. They're like secret

signals. They're saying, follow me,

follow me, follow meeeeeeeeee.

I guess I just walked right by the corner where Dad had turned because I was so busy following the tracks. I crossed a street, turned a corner, and kept following. Lines opened up into more lines. I followed one path through a grassy lot and came out behind a big building. There was a wooden fence, trash cans, and a rusty mattress spring. I looked up at the wall of the building. It was an office building with green windows all up and down its face. I wondered if someone had thrown the rusty mattress spring down from one of those green windows.

It was about then I realized I had got

myself lost. I followed my grass track
out to the street again. Dad and Mitch
and Robert were nowhere around, and I
was in a part of the city I'd never been
in before. Right next to the new office
building with green windows was a huge
lot with nothing on it but a big
billboard that said Urban Renewal. Some
kids were playing ball in a corner of
the lot. I found some tracks in the dirt
and kept following them. I was in the
section of town where black people live.
Across the street was a housing
development, rows and rows of three
story brick houses with little squares
of green in front, and clothes lines and
garbage pails on the concrete courtyards
in back.

Kids were playing everywhere. Some mothers were out in the backyards hanging clothes or talking or yelling at their little kids. Quite a few men had the hoods of their cars up and were working on them. Boys on bikes rode past me in herds.

"Out of the way, white girl!" one of them yelled, and he rode so close he snatched my beret and dropped it to the ground. Then he and all his friends he-hawed like a bunch of donkeys. Boys. I stuck out my tongue at them and plunked my beret back on my head. It's red to match my cape.

If I'd had somebody to walk with, I would have felt really happy. Around our

neighborhood, there are kids fooling
around, but not nearly as many as here,
and you hardly ever see the grownups
outside, just when they come out to
start up the power mowers and do the
lawns, or go shopping, or something. But
where I was, there was something to
look at every minute.

I stopped in a little store on the
corner and bought a candy bar. Then
somebody yelled my name.

"Trissy! Hey, Trissy baby!" It was
Patricia Crosby, one of the bus kids in
my classroom. She's a dark, tall skinny
girl with glasses. "What are you doing
here, baby?" she said.

"Walking around."

She put her arm through mine. "Well, I'll walk with you. Where you going?"

"No place special. Just walking and looking."

"Looking at what?" she said. She sounded mad all of a sudden.

"Everything," I said. I held out my candy bar. "Want a bite?"

"I'm allergic to chocolate," she said. "Also strawberries. I break out in a rotten rash. I itch everywhere, even on my behind."

That made me think of a funny story about my uncle Frank--the time he was out fishing and decided to take a swim and sat down in a patch of poison ivy to pull off his pants.

So we were both laughing, and
Patricia said, "Maybe we'll be friends."

"Maybe," I said. It's hard to be
friends with someone who lives across
the city from you.

"Want to eat lunch with me and Dolores
on Monday?" Patricia asked.

I thought about Steffi. Ever since she
said those things in gym class, she and
Laura Stegmeyer had gone everywhere and
done everything together. But maybe by
Monday she would want to be friends
again. What would I do then?

"I asked you something," Patricia
said. She sounded mad again.

"Yes, let's eat lunch together on

Monday," I said, and I was sorry I had
hesitated because Patricia didn't sound
as friendly again. Even so, we had a
good time, walking around, talking about
everyone and everything in school. She
told me she would like school a lot
better if there were at least a few
black teachers. I had never thought of
that before, and I tried to imagine
what it would be like for me to be in a
school with all black teachers, and no
white teachers. I decided that it
shouldn't make any difference, but it
probably would.

"How're you getting home?" she said at
last.

"I don't know if I ought to go home,

or go back downtown and try to find my father." I tried to explain to Pat how I'd wandered away from them, following the signs and tracks.

"You've got problems," she said, making the crazy sign on her forehead.

Right then, I realized I really did have problems. Daddy was probably boiling over right that instant.

"Why don't you go downtown--, it's not that far from here," Pat said. "Then you can find your pop or else take a bus home. Wait till I ask my mom if it's okay, and I'll walk you part way." I went to her house and waited outside while she checked with her mother. She

came out, eating an apple and carrying
one for me.

She walked me all the way back to the
library, then she went home, and I went
to the War Memorial. It looked like
about a million people milling around,
going in to see the show, and another
million coming out from seeing the show.
I stood on my toes and swung my head
back and forth, looking for Dad and
Mitch and Robert, till my neck ached. It
cost me a dollar to get into the show,
and I didn't have that much money. I
had 50 cents, though, and when I
couldn't see Dad or my brothers
anywhere, I went to Woolworths and

bought a hot dog. I wanted ice cream, too, but I needed bus fare home.

I always like taking the bus. I sat at a window and watched everything moving by. The starts and stops, the rumbles, creaks, and groans of the bus, the skeek, skeek of the doors opening and then shutting with a hot hissss made me feel goofy and a little bit sick and sort of floaty at the same time. And these goofy crazy things all tumbled around in my mind.

At the stop near my house, the driver said, "Okay, kid, are you getting off or not?" Because I was thinking, maybe I ought to keep riding the bus for a while

more. But I got off. I stopped at the
school playground. Some little kids were
on the swings. I thought about showing
them how to stand up and pump yourself
so high your feet point straight at the
sky.

A boy was trying to get a kite up into
the air. "Run, you dodo," I yelled. But
he just dumbly kept flopping the kite
along the ground.

If I'd had my jump rope, I would right
then and there have jumped 200 times
without missing.

But I had to go home.

Everyone was waiting for me. And they
all stared at me when I walked in.
"WHERE WERE YOU?" my mother said.

"She had candy," Robert said. "I can see chocolate on her face."

"We were getting ready to call the police," Dad said.

Only Mitch kept his mouth shut, just leaned against the wall with his arms folded, smirking his superior smirk.

I tried to explain what happened, but no matter what I said, they got mad.

"You went into _that_ section," Mom said. "Don't you have ANY sense?"

"Huh?" I said.

"Edith, let's not get into your narrow minded viewpoint," Dad said.

"Then you condone what she did?"

"No, I don't condone it! I'm good and mad at this girl. It was one of her

typically senseless actions. She had me
pretty worried! Well, Trissy Jane, what
did you expect to prove--in this
thoughtless way--your independence or
some other half-baked notion?"

"I told you, I just started following
lines--tracks--"

"Har, har, har," Mitch said. "I told
you she was cracked."

"Shut up! Make him shut up!"

"That's enough out of you, Mitch,"
Dad said. "You and Robert leave the
room. Now, Trissy Jane. What are we
going to do with you? You don't think
you can get away scot free with this
kind of behavior, do you?"

"Do you want to beat me?"

"Don't be stupid! Just sit there with your mouth shut for a change." After a lot more talk, he and Mom decided to suspend my allowance for a month this time, and give me more chores around the house. One of these days they're going to run out of punishments, and then what are they going to do?

DREAM NUMBER I

Last night I dreamed about Steffi's mother. In the dream she was wearing a beautiful blue dress and she had baked a huge orange cake for me. The cake had four candles on it for my birthday. Then Steffi wanted the cake, but her mother said NO, it was mine. Her mother's hair was long and floaty like Steffi's and she hugged me. Then I jumped into the cake and it was soft and squishy and everybody was laughing and feeling good.

When I woke up I felt so happy I wanted to visit Steffi's mother right away. But first I had to ask my mother's permission. I have to ask her permission

for EVERYTHING from now on, because of
wandering away from Dad and my brothers.

Uncle Arthur was over and he and Mom
were talking about taking a ride.
"Trissy, why don't you come with us?"
Uncle Arthur said. He took his pipe out
of his mouth and smiled his keen
friendly smile.

"No, thank you, Uncle Arthur. I want
to visit a friend."

"My, how polite," my mother said.
"What are you up to today, Trissy?" She
looked at Uncle Arthur and laughed. He
laughed his keen friendly laugh.

"Can I go over to the Jones'?" I said.

"May I?" my mother said.

"May I go over to the Jones'?"

"Well, I guess you'll be all right for a few hours. But no repeat performances on yesterday!"

"Yesterday. What happened yesterday?" Uncle Arthur said.

"Oh, Trissy went off and got herself lost and threw us all into a panic. Typical Trissy stuff. I tell you, I was shaking till she walked in that door." Then she put her hand on my head and sort of messed up my hair in a friendly way.

INSTRUCTIONS ON MAKING UP WITH YOUR
BEST FRIEND

1. Make the first move.

This is VERY important. Swallow your
pride, smile and say something friendly
like, "You're wearing a neat dress,
Steffi!" Even though you're in her house
and she doesn't answer, keep smiling in
a really friendly way.

2. Don't make dumb jokes about your
friend's new friend.

There must be <u>something</u> about Laura
Stegmeyer that's nice. Her frizzy
orange hair? Her speckled yellow eyes?
Or the way she squints in that keen,
super intelligent way?

3. Let your friend be FIRST in
everything.

Even when her own mother asks you to
choose the first piece of candy,
politely decline. "Steffi can go first."
Do the same thing in school. Don't wave
your hand in Mrs. Gilfer's face. Give
Steffi a chance to answer FIRST.

4. Give up something you really want
for friendship's sake.

Give up trying to be editor of the
sixth grade yearbook. Maybe lots of
people, including Steffi's own mother,
have told you you would be a good
editor, so what? Try not to smile like
an idiot when people say those things,
and instead point out that Steffi knows

how to get along with people a million
times better than you.

5. Use every opportunity to be
friendly and helpful to your friend.

Remember, friends laugh at the things
you laugh at, they like the things you
like, they're happy when you're happy,
and sad when you're sad. Friends are the
best things a person can have. So
MAKE UP with your best friend, NO
MATTER WHAT!

MRS. GILFER

English Class   I, TRISSY

Dialogue from Real Life

Setting: Playfound during recess.

Trissy: Hi, Steffi.

Steffi: Hi.

Trissy: Patricia and I were just going
across the street to the candy
store. You and Laura want to
come?

Steffi: There isn't enough time. The
bell's going to ring in a
minute. I love your dashiki,
Patricia.

Trissy: Those cookies your mother made
yesterday when I was visiting
were fabulous.

Steffi: Laura and I had them for lunch today. See, there's the bell ringing. Wait a minute, Trissy, let Pat and Laura and the others go ahead. I want to ask you something.

Trissy: You DO?

Steffi: Why did you come to my house yesterday?

Trissy: To see your mother. I like your mother. And to see you, too.

Steffi: I think you came to spy on me.

Trissy: What?

Steffi: You heard me. You came to spy, to see if Laura was over playing with me.

Trissy: I wouldn't care if Laura played

with you every day and every

night for the rest of the year.

Steffi: Why did you follow me all over

my house and give me all those

sickening smiles?

Trissy: I wouldn't care if Laura

Stegmeyer moved in with you.

Laura Stegmeyer. Ha. What's

Laura Stegmeyer to me? Nothing!

Steffi: You're jealous of Laura

Stegmeyer. You're so jealous it

sticks out all over your jealous

green face.

Trissy: Jealous of Laura Stegmeyer? Ha,

ha, ha, ha!

Steffi: And while I'm at it, I might

as well tell you I think the

way you act in school is disGUSting. You are always showing off and lying. Like today, telling Mrs. Gilfer in front of the whole class you didn't want to be class editor. You gave her one of your sickening smiles, and I know WHY. You were just lying, pretending to be so modest so Mrs. Gilfer would be impressed. I think it was a disGUSting trick!

Trissy: It was not a trick! I meant every word, but NOW I take it all back.

Steffi: Naturally! Because the truth is,

you want to be class editor so
bad you'd get down on your hands
and knees in front of the whole
world and BEG for it.

Trissy: Ha! Ha! The way YOU hang
around Mrs. Gilfer makes me
want to PUKE. All that extra
work you hand in. Your greedy
ambition to be class editor
sticks out all over your greedy
green face.

Steffi: Your voice is loud and UGLY,
and you're always raising your
hand and waving it in front of
everyone else. I don't care what
you say about me, I'm just
telling you all this for your

own GOOD, because we used to be best friends.

Trissy: I think you are the rottenest ASS I ever knew.

Steffi: That's another thing. Your disGUSting language. You're always saying disGUSting things just so you can make the boys laugh. And the way you dress! Different colored socks and--

Trissy: My socks are the same color today!

Steffi: ...and that cape you are always showing off in, and everything else. I really can't stand you, anymore.

Trissy: I not only can't stand you, you
ASS, I hate you. Goodby.

Steffi: Goodby! And good riddance to bad
rubbish. You are POLLUTION, and
please don't ever come near me
again.

Trissy: May God strike me DEAD if I ever
do.

THE MAD BAD TYPIST STRIKES AGAIN

and again!!!

evil words everywhere!!!

ass ass ASS ASSASS ASSSSSSS

fark farkfarkfarkfark FARK F-A-R-K!

falling from the clouds...chalked on the

sidewalks...oh those EVIL WORDS...he he

he...painted on the sides of buildings

...squigling down dark hallways...

sneaking around corners...

making mothers SHRIEK

and nicey nicey girls FAINT

oh phooey i hate my evil self

i'm going to see my father

RIGHT NOW!

Mom's gone to the market. Robert's with

her.

Mitch is supposed to be watchdogging me.

bow wow.

He's downstairs with the teevee.

I'm supposed to ask him if I want to go

somewhere.

Rats on that.

I think if a daughter wants to see her

father, she ought to be able to go see

him without asking permission, or

calling, or doing anything so dumb. She

ought to be able to just go see her

father.

so I'm going.

SECRET DOCUMENT # 22308398759387

Report to the President from Secret

Agent ITJB

Subject:

How Secret Agent ITJB got into her

father's locked apartment.

What Secret Agent ITJB did in her

father's apartment.

Why Secret Agent ITJB went beserk

before she left.

THIS MEMO IS HIGHLY CONFIDENTIAL.

SECRET   SECRET   SECRET

SECRET   SECRET   SECRET

Secret Agent ITJB left her home at

exactly 3:42 p.m. and proceeded to Oak

Street, where her father now resides.

She walked 57 blocks and by the time she rang the doorbell of Mitchell Beers in the downstairs hall, her feet really hurt.

Oooh, did they ever. And what was worse--all the way over, I was thinking Dad would give me a ride home, and then he didn't even answer the bell. I kept ringing and ringing. I didn't want to walk home 57 blocks. I rang some more. Suddenly this guy with wiry hair came charging out into the hall, yelling. "Knock it off, kid! Knock it off!"

I said I was here to see my father and he lived in this house.

He said, "Go see the super and stop

ringing that stupid bell!"

So I rang the bell that said
superintendent. A baldheaded man
answered the door. "Yesss?" he said. He
had a toothpick in the corner of his
mouth.

"Excuse me," I said, "I'm Mitchell
Beers' daughter and he isn't home. I
want to wait for my father. Do you know
who could let me into his apartment?"

"Yessss." He flipped the toothpick
from one end of his mouth to the other.

"Well, could you tell me who that is?"

"Yessssss."

"Who is it, please?"

"Me."

"Well, would you please let me in?"

He folded his arms across his chest.
"Why?"

"Why what?"

"Why should I let you in?"

I was beginning to think that everyone
in this house was slightly crazy.
"Because I'm Mitchell Beers' daughter
and he isn't home, and I'd like to go
into his apartment and wait for him!"

"How do I know you're really Beers'
daughter? Maybe you're a thief."

"ME?" I nearly screeched. I was so
mad I stamped my foot, even though it
was a truly juvenile thing to do. I went
to the door and yanked it open, thinking
about those 57 blocks I had to walk back
home, and how the whole trip had been a
big fat ZERO.

"Hey, Beers' daughter. Come on!" He twitched his finger at me. He jungled a bunch of keys on a metal ring. "I'll let you in."

I followed him up the stairs, and I started hearing this story in my head. Once upon a time, Trissy went to see her father, and this mad killer disguised as the janitor let her in.

By the time we got to a really dark part of the hall, I was afraid it was going to be goodby, Trissy.

He put his clammy hands with the filthy long nails around her slender neck, and squeezed....

"Mr. Christopher!" A woman wearing

pink fuzzy bedroom slippers, with pink rollers in her hair, popped out of her apartment. "Mr. Christopher! Just the man I want to see!"

"Busy now," the super said.

"But, Mr. Christopher," Pink Lady pouted, "you promised to look at my sink a whole week ago. It leaks constantly!"

"Busy now," he said again. He turned the corner and twitched his finger at me.

"But Mr. Christopher!"

I followed him up the next flight, thinking that Pink Lady had saved me from being strangled on the second floor, but who was going to save me on the third floor?

Ha, ha, ha, the mad killer laughed
hollowly. Trissy tried to scream, but
everything was turning black.

"Beers' daughter!" He was holding open
a door. "This is it."

I slid in past his outstretched arm.
Just when she thought she was safe, he
lunged for her soft exposed throat.
"Thanks," I sort of squeaked.

He nodded. "Tell your Daddy it was
your idea to have me let you in. And,
Beers' daughter, if you don't wait for
him, be sure to lock when you go out."
He shut the door.

I looked around. I'd been in my
father's apartment only once before
when he first moved in. I'd wanted to

come again, but there was always some
reason I couldn't. Either he was busy,
or Mom said I was, or he said everything
was in a mess and no place for a girl.

There were newspapers spread on the
navy blue couch. First I sat down. I
picked up a newspaper. Then I put it
down and looked around some more. I
hummed to myself. I noticed an ashtray
practically choking with cigarette
butts. I picked up a butt and stuck it
in my mouth. Then some of the tobacco
got on my tongue and tasted really bad.
I spit it out and wondered when Dad
would be home. Then I got the idea of
cleaning up.

I jumped up and folded all the

newspapers neatly together and stacked
them on a corner table. I emptied three
ashtrays and wiped them clean with the
sleeve of my sweater. There were books
everywhere, even on the floor. I
gathered them up and stacked them into
the bookcase near the hall door.

After that I went into the bedroom. It
was as bare as the livingroom. A bed, a
bureau, and two chairs. No curtains, no
rugs, no pictures on the walls. Just
Dad's hairbrush and some loose change on
the bureau. I got a sad feeling,
thinking how pretty everything is at
home. I wondered if Dad missed it. I
pulled up the shade and looked out the
window. Down on the street, there were

cars, cars, and more cars. And Dad
always said he hated traffic.

I went into the bathroom. I opened
the medicine cabinet and took down
Dad's jar of Noxema, which he uses for
shaving. I liked the smell. Since he
moved out, I really miss that smell.
Mitch doesn't have any beard yet, and
when he does grow one, he'll probably
be so contrary he wouldn't use Noxema
for shaving if you offered him a million
dollars.

The sink didn't look too clean, but I
really hate scrubbing sinks. Mom's
always trying to get me to scrub the
bathroom sink, or the kitchen sink. I
looked at the can of cleanser, sprinkled

a little on the sink, yawned, and put
the cleanser back under the sink. I ran
water and swished it around. Even for my
father, I didn't see what difference it
made if the sink was clean or not.

Next I decided to go into the kitchen.
There's always dishes, pots, and things
to wash or wipe in a kitchen. I don't
like washing dishes either, but if I did
Daddy's dishes, he'd see how useful I
could be. Then he'd say, "Why, Trissy,
now I know what's been missing in my
life. YOU. Why don't you come live with
me?"

I was so struck by this perfect idea
that I stopped dead in the doorway
between the livingroom and the kitchen

so I could see the whole thing happening
in my mind. I could see Dad's face and
the way he'd push his hand back over his
head when he said it. "Why, Trissy!
What's the matter with me? I must have
been blind all these months! You have
to come live with me. Your mother has
the two boys, so she won't be lonely.
It's only fair that I have at least one
of my children!" Then he'd whisper in
my ear, "Anyway, you were always my
favorite. Of all the children, I've
missed YOU the most. Yes, the very
most."

I felt so bubbly and light thinking
that, I decided I would wash a whole
sinkful of dishes, and then go into the

bathroom and scrub the sink and the tub, too!

Then I saw the cake.

It was set in the middle of the kitchen table, a two layer cake with chocolate fudge frosting running down the sides. I didn't touch it. I bent close and sniffed. It smelled fresh. All along, I had wondered what that good smell in the apartment was. There was a folded note slipped under the plate the cake was on. I picked it up and read it.

"MITCHY,

I came down with a severe case of domesticity this morning and decided I should do something positive with
- it. Let myself in and cleaned up the

kitchen. Still feeling positively

domestic. Hence, freshly baked,

homemade (NO mixes!) cake. Hope you

like it!!!!!!!!!

Call me tonight.

                      Yours, G."

I folded the note very carefully and

put it back where I found it. I didn't

plan to gc out of my mind. I didn't do

it on purpose. It just happened.

I plunged both hands into the cake,

all ten fingers. The cake was still warm

inside. I squeezed and mashed it until

it was all over the table top. Then I

gathered gobs of chocolate fudge

frosting in my hands. I smeared hand

prints of frosting on the kitchen walls,
through the livingroom, and out into the
hall. Maybe I was laughing when I did
it. Maybe I was crying. I thought, _Boy_,
this _sure_ _is_ _a_ _disgusting_ _mess_, but I
couldn't stop. I even smeared fudge
frosting on the bannister going down the
stairs. Then I walked home. 57 blocks.

MEDICAL REPORT

Patient: Trissy Jane Beers

The patient has been thoroughly examined and the chocolate cake episode discussed at some length. Patient freely admits her guilt, but says she doesn't know why she went beserk.

Recommend that patient be put into a funny farm and the key thrown away.

In plain words, she is a nut. A fruitcake. A loony.

(signed) Dr. U. R. A. Kookoo.

LAST WILL AND TESTAMENT

I, Trissy, being of sound mind and body now write my last will and testament, in case by morning I'm dead.

To Steffi Jones, my ex best friend, I leave my Nancy Drew collection as proof that friendship goes beyond the grave.

To my brother Robert I leave my Monopoly game since he's already stolen all the red hotels.

My brother Mitch probably doesn't want anything I have. I will leave him the two dollars, 43¢ in my elephant bank.

That's it. These are the only people I care about in the whole world, and anybody I left out will realize I left

them out on purpose. If people don't
care about me, why should I care about
them?

I, Trissy

MULTIPLE CHOICE MURDER TEST

(choose one)

Let Daddy's friend "G":

A - Choke on chocolate cake.

B - Drown in a pool of mud.

C - Get locked in a pen with an enraged
     bull when she's wearing a red dress.

Dear Dumb Beers,

Do you remember, Stupid, when you were about 4 years old and you got into Mitch's stamp collection and messed it all up?

In the middle of the night, he crept into your room and woke you up. He said, "I'm going to fix you for messing my stamp collection. I'm taking you to the swamp and I'm leaving you there with all the little slimy biting, crawling, creepy things that will EAT you up and just leave your bare bones!"

I pulled the covers over my head. I was so scared I didn't even dare breath. I stayed under the covers until I almost suffocated. Then I poked out my nose and discovered Mitch was gone. But I hardly slept all night, thinking that any minute he might come back and drag me off to that swamp.

The next day Mom made Mitch admit he was just threatening me. All he'd wanted to do was scare me into being good. And he did. I never touched his stamp collection again.

When Mom and Dad separated, I thought it was like the swamp--just a threat, a horrible period of time like those suffocating minutes under the covers, and the best thing was not to think about it too much. Then it would be over sooner, and we'd be back to normal.

Was I really so stupid?

Way in the back of my mind, didn't I know better? Didn't I know their separation was for real and for good?

That's the trouble with me, anyway.

I tell myself too many stories.

So, Dumb Beers, do you think you can remember now the way things are?

Are you wide awake this time, Stupid? Open your eyes.

I'm telling you all this for your own good,

Dummy.

Yours in Truth,

I, Trissy

P.S. From now on, stick to the facts.

P.P.S. Just the FACTS, and only the

FACTS, and nothing but the FACTS.

P.P.P.S. NO MORE MAKE BELIEVE.

HOW THE FIRE BEGAN

1. I sneaked into Mitch's room and took
   a book of matches, which he is not
   supposed to have, but does, because
   he is smoking secretly. He keeps his
   matches in his off limits desk
   drawer. (I didn't look at his dumb,
   naked girl books.)

2. I took Nancy Drew collection.

3. I took chewed up stuffed mouse Dad
   gave me during stuffed mouse phase.

4. I took old drawings and stories from
   third, fourth, and fifth grade (which
   I had been saving for when I got
   famous, to show that even as a mere
   child I had superb talent--ha ha)

5. I took china cat Mom gave me during china cat phase.

6. I dumped everything into my large plastic wastebasket. (My big mistake.)

7. I dropped a lighted match into the basket. Drawings and stories went WHOOOSH! into flames. Everything else went sputter.

8. I poked up the fire a bit with my back scratcher. (Mitch's generous 25¢ Christmas gift.)

9. Everything went gooey and soft, and a great big cloud of thick, dark grey smoke funneled up.

WHAT HAPPENED NEXT

1. I was coughing like mad. The cloud
   of smoke (which stunk like a skunk)
   was rolling toward the door. I tried
   to shoo it to the window. No luck.

2. Loud noises from the hallway.
   Banging on my door. Mom burst in.
   Uncle Arthur was right behind her.

3. Mom shrieked. "Trissy! What are you
   doing? My God, the room is on fire!"

4. Uncle Arthur pushed Mom aside and
   stamped on the smoldering, stinking
   mess of plastic, books, and stuffed
   mouse, getting his shiny black
   buckle boots covered with goo.

5. Mother called me thoughtless,

stupid, irresponsible, and immature.
"Idiot!" She grabbed my arm and
shook me. "You could have set our
house on fire, and killed us all!"

6. She shook me so hard, my teeth
started chattering.

7. Uncle Arthur said, "Edith, dear.
Please. I'm sure she didn't realize
...her side of the story...
thoughtless, but...just a child...
difficult...adjustment..."

8. Mom began crying. "I don't know, I
don't know." She put her hands up to
her face.

9. Uncle Arthur put his arm around her.
"Maybe you should say something to
your mother, Trissy. There must be

some explanation. How did it happen? Why did you do it?"

10. I said, "It was like the chocolate fudge frosting on the wall."

11. "Chocolate fudge frosting?" my mother said. She sounded like she was going to start screaming again. "Chocolate fudge frosting! What's the child talking <u>about</u>!"

12. Uncle Arthur said, "Edith."

13. Mom said, "Yes, yes, all right." Her nose was red. "I'll control myself."

HOW I FELT BECAUSE OF WHAT I DID

1. Hard for me to breathe.

2. As if a rock was pressed down on my chest.

3. Stupid and sorry.

4. Dumber than dumb.

5. Tired. Wished I could get into bed, pull the covers over my head, and never come out.

WHAT HAPPENED AFTERWARDS

1. "Trissy," my mother said. "Turn around and look at me." She looked so unhappy, I started to bawl. Uncle Arthur's friendly smile got completely unhooked. I was hiccuping and burping. "I'm sorry, I didn't mean to scare you, I didn't want to set our house on fire," I babbled. "I just wanted to get rid of some baby junk, and everything went wrong. Everything always goes wrong."

2. My mother took me in her arms. She held my head against her breast and petted my head. "My poor baby," she said.

3. I was so surprised I stopped crying, hiccuping, and burping. My mother gave a big sigh. "It hasn't been easy for you, has it, Trissy? And now I'm going to tell you something else. I don't know if it will make things better or worse for you. But you have to know."

4. Uncle Arthur was biting on his pipe. "That's right, tell her everything, Edith. The sooner told, the sooner the adjustment." And then _he_ told me. "Your mother and I are going to be

married after your parents' divorce
is final." His friendly smile was
hooked into place again. "Well,
Trissy, how are you going to like
having me as a stepfather?"

5. "Sure, that would be okay," I said.
My mother and Uncle Arthur looked
happy. They didn't ask me, and I
didn't tell them, but if it was up to
me, I wouldn't choose _him_ for a
stepfather, or "G" (whoever _she_ is)
for a stepmother.

Dear Father,

I am in quarantine as a punishment.
Did Mother tell you what I did this
time? Probably.

I want to ask you something. When Mom
marries Uncle Arthur, she will be Edith
Bronson Beers Jobaggy. What will I be?
I mean, who will I be?

Your daughter,

Trissy.

P. S. Did the chocolate fudge frosting
clean off okay? I hope so. I'm
sorry.

TELEPHONE TALK

- Hello. Is this Trissy Jane Beers?

- Yes. Who is this, please?

- This is your father, Mitchell Powell Beers.

- Dad! How funny! What a funny way to talk to me.

- Trissy, I want to tell you something very serious, actually, and I want you to listen to me.

- Okay, Dad.

- Are you still in quarantine, by the way?

- Yes, mostly I am.

- Well, I'm going to speak to your mother about that. I think things are

going to change, don't you? I mean,
the way you feel about things and
act, and--

- I guess so. I mean, I hope so.
- Well, don't cry, honey. We all make
mistakes, and yours are just childish
ones. Now listen to me. Here's what I
want to tell you. You, when you were
born, were named by your mother and
me. Now you've heard that story enough
times. How much we wanted a girlbaby,
and how happy we were, how very happy.
And how I sat with your mother in the
hospital and called out all sorts of
girls' names. Like 'Pamela, come
here!' 'Shirley, eat your oatmeal!'
And at last I said, 'Trissy, behave

yourself!' And your mother and I
agreed that was the perfect name for
our baby. For you. And we added Jane
because it sounded nice with Trissy.
Fancy and plain, I remember your
mother saying. And then Beers, because
children get their father's last
names--

- I know all that, Daddy.
- Sure you do. Well, the point is,
honey, you are Trissy Jane Beers, no
matter what your mother and I do.
That's the name you were born with.
That's who you are, and that's what
you're always going to be till you get
married someday--
- I know all that, too, Daddy.

- Good. Think about it. When you have
  trouble, it doesn't make you a
  different person, or less of a person,
  or no person. You are still you. Your
  name is still Trissy Jane Beers. It
  is yours, and whatever that name
  stands for is up to you. Whatever
  people think of when they hear that
  name depends on you. How you act, how
  you talk, how you dress, what you do.
  Get it?
- Yes.
- It doesn't depend on your mother and
  me, or anyone else, because you are a
  separate person. You are yourself. You
  are an individual. Do you understand,
  Trissy Jane Beers?

- Yes.

- Good. Don't forget.

- I won't.

FRIENDS RE-UNITED

QUARRELS FORGOTTEN

(Trissy Press International)

May 20. Jefferson City

Trissy J. Beers, and Steffi T.
Jones, both members of the sixth
grade graduating class of Jefferson
Elementary School on Spring
Road, today buried the hatchet
and made up their long series
of quarrels.

In separate interviews, both Miss
Jones and Miss Beers told this
reporter they were delighted at
this newest turn of events.

"Actually, it was all so stupid,"
said Miss Jones.

"Well, I'm glad, even though I also have other best friends now," said Miss Beers, referring to Miss Patricia Crosby who accompanied her to the interview.

Asked to comment about the root cause of their vicious quarrels both Miss Jones and Miss Beers said, 'No comment.'

Dear Diary,

Mrs. Gilfer says a diary is invaluable. With just a few words to jolt our memories, years from now we can look back and remember so much.

Steffe, Laura, Pat and I ate lunch together today. I had half of Patricia's peanut butter sandwich because I forgot my lunch. Steffi contributed a piece of pound cake (which she despises) and Laura graciously gave me a dill pickle. Still don't like her thrillingly much.

Steffi wrote me a note in Montgomery's class. "Beers, it was boring these weeks without you."

I wrote her back. "Jones, not for me."

Mrs. Dilfer said I should by all rights be editor of the yearbook, but since the other kids voted for Steffi's creative effort, democracy would have to prevail.

"Still you must help Steffi all you can," she said. She adjusted her false bosoms. "Steffi is so pretty, but prettiness isn't enough, you know. Now THERE'S a good subject for a story, I'missy."

She is always giving me good subjects for stories. She thinks I want to be a writer when I grow up. But what I really want to be, I decided, is a nurse. Patricia's mother is a nurse, and she wants to be a nurse, and we've agreed to go to nurses' training together. Steffi and Laura

still don't know what
they want to be, which
I think is rather dumb
of them.

More tomorrow.

Yrs. Truly, dear Diary,
Prissy Jane Beers